TWO KITTIES

Julia Crow Haberler

First Printing: 2016
ISBN 978-1-365-49395-9
New Castle, Colorado

www.twokittiesbook.com

For Ellie,

who thinks kitties are the best

TWO. KITTIES START THE DAY

ONE KITTY WANTS TO PLAY

KITTY KITTY TOO

TWO KITTIES HAVE A SNACK

KITTY ONE PREPS FOR ATTACK

TWO KITTIES IN THE SUN

THIS KITTY HAS SOME FUN

TWO KITTIES HAVE A NAP

BUT THERE WAS A
SLIGHT MISHAP

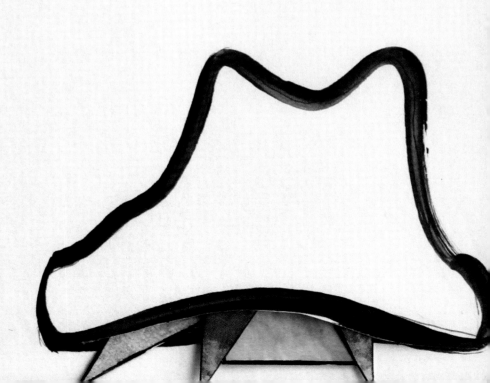

TWO KITTIES HAVE A DRINK

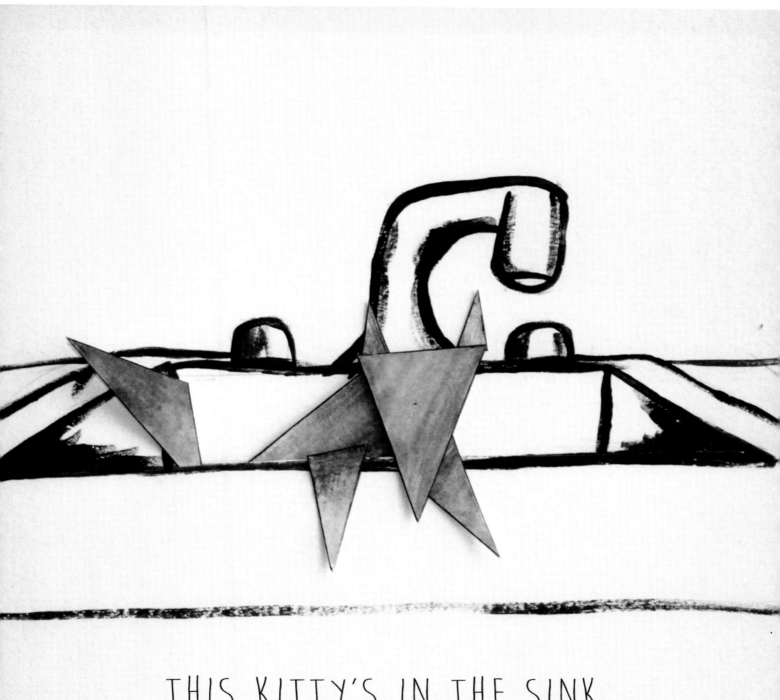

THIS KITTY'S IN THE SINK

TWO KITTIES STRETCH OUT LONG

ONE KITTY SINGS A SONG

TWO KITTIES WAY UP HIGH

GRAVITY TEST:
NUMBER FOUR HUNDRED SIXTY FIVE

TWO KITTIES

HAVE A BATH

THE CURTAINS
FACE THE
AFTERMATH

TWO KITTIES LOOK OUT THE WINDOW

THAT LAMP WAS IN THE WAY

SO WAS THIS PLANT

AND THE TOILET PAPER

AND THIS BOOK

NO, TWO KITTIES!

THIS IS WHY WE CAN'T HAVE NICE THINGS

THE END